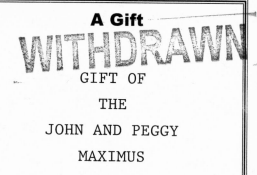

Copyright © 2008 by Kazuno Kohara
Published by Roaring Brook Press
Roaring Brook Press is a division of Holtzbrinck Publishing Holdings Limited Partnership
175 Fifth Avenue, New York, New York 10010
www.roaringbrookpress.com
Published in Great Britain by Macmillan Children's Books, London
All rights reserved

Distributed in Canada by H. B. Fenn and Company Ltd.

Cataloging-in-Publication Data is on file at the Library of Congress
ISBN: 978-1-59643-427-1

Roaring Brook Press books are available for special promotions and premiums.
For details contact: Director of Special Markets, Holtzbrinck Publishers.

First American Edition August 2008
Printed in November 2009 in Belgium by PROOST, Turnhout, Antwerp
5 7 9 8 6 4

Ghosts in the House!

Kazuno Kohara

ROARING BROOK PRESS
NEW YORK

Once there was a girl who went to live in a big old house at the edge of town. It was a splendid place, but there was one problem.

SOLD

The house was . . .

...haunted!

But the girl wasn't just a girl.

She was a witch!